The Lane to Paradise

To Suzanne

with love from

Margaret

Dorking, August 2016

The Lane to Paradise

Felix
A Celebration

India Russell

CAPSTICK & WAGG

Capstick & Wagg
Dorking
www.capstickandwagg.co.uk

ISBN 978-0-9930440-0-7

Acknowledgements are due to the editors of Stacey International,
Godstow Press and *Acumen* who first published some of these poems;
also to the Reverend Kevin Scott
for permission to include his
Ask Jasper letter to Felix, *Old Malden News*.

Typeset, printed and bound by
www.taylorthorneprint.co.uk

CONTENTS

ILLUSTRATIONS

FELIX 1990–2013

For twenty three years Felix has been my constant companion – a source of peace and reassurance. Even in his last few days when he could no longer move or eat, he would greet me with his special loving chirrup. The night before he died (for his last few days I slept beside him in the drawing room on a camp bed) when I got up to cuddle him and make him comfortable, he purred in his old reassuring way and it was though everything was all right and a great feeling of peace came over me and I slept as I had never slept before; and all the following day, while Michael sat with him on his lap, the same peace was with me and all stress seemed to disappear and all nagging worries. It was as though he were giving me one final and significant lesson. And I kept thinking of Socrates, still teaching whilst he was slowly dying.

Felix was so positive in his outlook. He loved life and his various homes and gardens and all the natural world. He was a peace maker (he never hunted although he would occasionally make funny disgruntled noises when blackbirds didn't appreciate his presence). He was a peace maker even to the extent of rattling his cat flap so loudly and persistently if an arguement was going on that we had to stop. In the Winter he loved sitting with me on the sofa by the fire and listening to the turning pages of a book or writing pad, or the gentle buzz of conversation which he would occasionally join in with an affirmative miaow or purr. And he was always convivial at parties – once pouncing on the *Monopoly* money which, as banker, I had neatly set out on the chaise and then, as I wrested it from under his paws, snatching it away from me as I tried to hand it out! (As a spiritual being he would, of course, be opposed to bankers and money lenders!)

Often, early in the morning, when I was writing in bed, he would become covered in sheets of paper until I had what I thought was the final draft and then I would say, having uncovered him, 'What do you think of this, Felix?' and read it to him. And always he gave some response, purring or snuggling up in a circle or blinking his eyes at me.

For Lucy also, he was a great guide and friend. She came to us as a very disturbed cat, having been cruelly treated. (It took her about five years before she could cross an open space.) But Felix adopted her, and although she professed independence and was very different from Felix she followed him – though she would pretend, for example, that she was really only taking the same route in the garden as Felix, just a few minutes later, because she chose to!

When Lucy died five years ago Felix mourned. Soon after Michael had buried her under the laurels at the bottom of the garden I was standing on the terrace when Felix came out of the french windows and, without acknowledging me, walked deliberately down the steps and down to the shubbery where he disappeared for quite a while. We had not had time to show him Lucy's grave but that must have been where he was for he slowly retraced his path through the garden and up the steps onto the terrace and then, standing near me and looking down towards the shrubbery, he gave the most heart-rending howl of lamentation I have ever heard.

The E.T.A. Hoffmann quote about cats and animals in one of Felix's 'letters' is so true. They <u>are</u> wise. They know things that our small compass of intelligence could never know.

The Lane to Paradise

Felix
A Celebration

I dedicate this collection to
all those who work to alleviate the
suffering of animals and their environment
and foster a respect for Nature

The Lane to Paradise

Sometimes, dwelling in our quiet
Companionship, my spirit wandering
Through a maze of memories and dreams,
Dear Felix suddenly purrs so loudly,
Turning round to look into my eyes,
It seems as though he's there
Within my musing.

It happened again today when,
Far away in Devon,
In the lane to Paradise from *Whidown*
I gradually found his purring presence with me
There, beneath the rain-dark shining trees,
Shafts of sudden sunlight
Lighting up his fur, the raindrops and the stream,
Gilding the lilting deer and chasing squirrels
With magic and with mystery.

And I wondered if my sage companion,
Who never in reality knew *Whidown*,
Had seen the beauty of my vision,
And was pleased to be there, with me,
Walking along the lane to Paradise.

****

[*Whidown* was my family home for many years and Paradise was the lovely copse bordering on our grounds; the seat and table where I wrote the final draft of *They all knew* came from *Whidown* as did the rhododendron behind me, over Felix's grave.]

Gertie the Theatre Cat,
Phoenix Theatre, London
c/o *The Stage*

Dorking, 1992

Dear Gertie,

We were SO pleased to read your letter in this week's *Stage* saying that, despite former opposition from a few silly people (who obviously are completely insensitive), you were continuing at the Phoenix as Resident Theatre Cat. A vital member of the back stage crew may we add! And, of course, a great comfort to the actors!

Ever since India, the somewhat over-sensitive actress with whom share a house, drew our attention to the upsetting article, 'Phoenix targets the feeline for Gertie', p.16 Oct.20th.', we have been worried about you. We thought of sending some books on the human psyche but then we thought you might be too busy to read, and food would have looked like charity. Humans are uncertain creatures – they get so worked up and irritable about the oddest things. You should hear India on the difficulties of her profession and the problems super-star-status humans give her. They seem to lack the breadth, grace and philosophical nature of we felines. But they can't help it; it's all to do with breeding and evolution and we must do all we can to help them by keeping them amused and happy. I know we do. We distract India with silly games like 'ambush-leaps', 'ping-pong through the rug tunnel', 'pawball on the stairs' and the like for hours on end and she's always calmer afterwards. We're exhausted of course but it's all in a day's work. Have you ever tried giving them acupuncture with the front paws – excellent for frayed nerves, especially when accompanied by loud, regular purring.

But we mustn't ramble on. This was just a quick line to say we are so pleased you're well – emotionally as well as physically, and we know India is. She worries about us all so much that she can't concentrate on her acting and that would never do – because she's not bad, although we do have to leave the room sometimes when she gets too loud. Felix once jumped on her shoulder to stop her crying (he thought it was about animals) but then he realised she was acting – 'Hedvig' actually from her Dance Drama *The Secret Rooms of the Mind - Ibsen's Spiritual Evolution* – so it *was* about animals really. I seem to remember the tearful words, *'because I say prayers for the wild duck every evening, and pray for her to be protected from death and everything that is horrible.'* She must have been a nice girl. Anyway Felix felt a bit embarrassed to have made India jump by his jump! – but she didn't seem to mind, in fact she gave him a big cuddle-thankyou! I think she was pleased to be back as herself again! Funny business acting, as you must well know!

There we go again, rambling.

Lots of love to you, Gertie. May your coat be shining and bright and your purring (and perhaps acupuncture?) bring lots of delight,

from two feline friends (cousins perhaps?),

Felix and Lucy,
Kwetu Studio

My gentle Prince

My gentle prince from a far countree
Sings to me of sky and sea
Of grottos cool and forests deep
Where ancient Druids their watches keep.

He whispers, when I'm feeling low,
Of wondrous things and pathways bright
That lead beyond this dolorous place
To palaces of Truth and Grace.

He warms me when I'm feeling cold
And hums and murmurs tales of old
Lying beside me on my bed
He tells me things that can't be said

And often as I drift to sleep
I wonder at such Protean skill
That allows my gentle, prince so wise
To assume a furry, feline guise.

Wonder

Felix is dreaming of the willow tree.
Last evening, as the wind arose,
He lay beneath its streaming branches
Staring up into its greeny vaults

And as the wind caught one and then another
Weeping strand, he played with it as with
a friend,
His feline eyes the colour of the leaves,
His flowing grace an echo of the tree's.

And I, a poor observer of this mystery,
Stand yet again, unlike the master cat,
A novice on the threshold of philosophy
Which, for us both, begins with wonder.

The Circle of Love

And still the messengers come,
    Sailing through the battering waves of poison
                the cacophony of machines
                and man's degenerate world,

The holy birds

Sparrows, seeming gleeful, hymn among the waste while,
Disregarding chainsaws, trees tower heavenwards with
Their glorious chorus;

The divine Sun still shines and, through the deadly blanket
Of man's persistent clamour, his rays light up
A little corner unsullied by the flood of human greed –

A book telling of better worlds to come
Marked with a fading letter written when all seemed hopeful,
The chair now occupied by a cat
Curled in an eternal circle

                His gentle purr replying to the
                Touching rays and returning
                To Apollo his pure warmth
                In understanding reciprocity.

The Struggle

In the silent watches of the night
My clamorous thoughts sing out
Discordantly
And in my fruitless efforts to achieve some
Harmony, I lose myself in tortuous
Corridors of waking dreams, where
Shadows of what had once been shining thought
Loom up and almost overpower me, their dark
Dissembling forms mocking my visions of
The Eternal Realm of Truth and Beauty;

and were it not
For this so princely cat purring beside me
Like a faithful guardian from that Realm of
Light, occasionally glimpsed with joyful recognition,
more real far than
The ignoble, trying world which ever knocks me down,

I would
Give up the bruising struggle and surrender
To that most horrible Gorgon of the mind, despair.

When my Lion Roars

to Felix, rescue cat who ever rescues me

When my lion roars he roars with laughter
And when he jumps he always jumps for joy

For seeing, as he does,
The lives of humans – so full
Of tangled thoughts and rush and care,
He thanks his dear Divinity
He is a feline with the gift
Of Stillness, who can stare

And merge into the Wonder of all Nature
Become as one with all the tingling World
And then give praise to the Creator
Singing with every holy breath he takes.

Often, so quietly and so kindly,
He looks at me and says, 'Don't worry – I am here.
Forget the silly world of humans
That ever hurts and makes you sad and drear.
Just laugh at its so selfish petty foibles
And then, together, we can contemplate the All.'

And once, in such companionable silence,
He turned and looked down deep into my eyes and,
With a roar of laughter, then said quietly,
'Do you know, you're almost like a cat!'

Yes, when my lion roars he roars with laughter
And when he jumps he always jumps for joy.

Worcester Park, 18th. December, 2007

Dear Fuchsi,

I was very pleased with your photograph this morning – I can see that you would appreciate the poem *When my lion roars*. I am, in fact, not a lion, she's wrong there, but of course India is a poet and one has to make allowances – they see things in a different way (rather as we do). However, I do have a handsome mane (or ruff), although I say it myself – but it would seem that I'm a Norwegian Forest Cat and I must say that when I sit on India's desk when she is reading Ibsen, I have no difficulty at all with the language and, in fact, find I am quite fluent. As for the Forest part, I am quite content, having moved now with India, Michael and Lucy (another rescue cat who can be very wearing) three times – quite content, as I say, with our fairly substantial garden in which there are some sizeable trees and shrubs and, in the Summer, some very comfortable chairs from where one can 'contemplate the All', which, of course, one does not get in a forest, Norwegian or otherwise!

À propos names, mine is also German although it is usually pronounced in the English way. A funny story – India was at a 'posh' party in Dorking when Lucy and I lived there as kittens and someone at this party said to India that 'Felix' was a very common name for a cat. And completely out of the blue (she had never thought of the name before!) she found herself answering, 'Actually it's Felix Bartholdy Mendelssohn' (pronouncing it in the German way & cleverly reversing the surname) 'but we call him Felix for short.' I roared with laughter when she told me, and even Lucy smiled; apparently the chap seemed quite put out and walked off! – so humourless some humans aren't they?

I'll ask India to sort out some photographs of me in return for yours but I think they are in the loft – and it may be some time – so I'd better try and describe myself. 'Long-haired Tabby' is what I hear myself described as, but I would say that I am a philosopher of many years, clad in a fine striped cloak in shades of grey and black and a rather beautiful beige colour with a little white, long and luxuriant whiskers, a very bushy tail and having a very fine and noble face (and a curly tummy!). My purr is gentle and my thoughts deep. Like India, I dream a lot and I think we sometimes dream of each other, especially when I sleep on her bed which is nearly every night. (Quite a good bed, actually.) Much of her poetry, of course, comes from that wondrous realm we both sail off to so often.

Before I finish this I must ask you if you have read *Lebensansichten des Kater Murr* by E.T.A. Hoffmann – very amusing and so true. Why humans think they are so clever I do not know. Where would they be without us!? A quote therefrom:

'Indem ich', sprach Kreisler 'diesen klugen Kater betrachte, fällt es mir wieder schwer aufs Herz, in welchen engen Kreis unsere Erkenntnis gebannt ist. – Wer kann es sagen, wer nur ahnen, wie weit das Geistesvermögen der Tiere geht! – Wenn uns etwa oder vielmehr alle in der Natur unerforschlich bleibt, so sind wir gleich mit Namen bei der Hand und brüsten uns mit unserer albernen Schulweisheit, die eben nicht viel weiter reicht als unsere Nase. So haben wir denn auch das ganze geistige Vermögen der Tiere, das sich oft auch die wunderbarste Art äußert, mit der Bezeichnung Instinkt abgefertigt. Ich möchte aber nur die einzige Frage beantwortet haben, ob mit der Idee des

Instinkts, des blinden, willkürlosen Triebes, die Fähigkeit zu traümen vereinbar sei.'

Murr (Homme de lettres très renommé)

Lebensansichten des Kater Murr Erster Band. Erster Abschnitt

('Whilst I' said Kreisler, 'observe this wise cat, it again deeply worries me in what a narrow circle our faculty of perception is confined. – Who can tell, who can even sense, how far the spiritual power of animals goes. When for us, some, or even more, all in Nature remains impenetrable, then we immediately have a name to hand and preen ourselves with our silly school-knowledge which certainly does not go much further than our nose. In the same way we have also dispatched with the whole spiritual power of animals, which often expresses itself in the most wonderful way, with the label 'instinct'. But I would like just the one single question answered: whether the idea of instinct, the blind non-discretionary impulse, is compatible with the ability to dream.'

Murr (Homme de lettres très renommé))

Tom Cat Murr's Views on Life First Volume. First Passage)

translation: India Russell

Not bad writing is it and, of course, so true. Humans are so quick to label and dismiss! (Even Eliot – T.S., agrees!) I, in fact, had not read this for many years and only looked it up to check the title after having written the previous paragraph about dreaming and then found this very passage marked with exclamation marks!! And the telling sentence , 'So haben wir ..... mit der Bezeichnung abgefertigt.' ! Such a pattern there is in Life, if only the silly humans (and in this category I of course do not include Jack Herbert, E.T.A.Hoffmann, India Russell, and those other Enlightened Ones who recognise us) did not try so hard to wreck it!

Following on from this, have you read *Wonder* in *The Kaleidoscope of Time*, which I inspired? The philosophy reference is, of course, Aristotle. But I don't need to tell you that – not a bad poem.

Well I really must go now as I have a lot of things to attend to, being Christmas – inspect the tree (I'm pleased to say that they do not have a real one), say hello to the Nürnberger Flitterengel keeping watch on top, as she has every Christmas I can remember, count the presents and decide which one I will sleep on, have a few words with Lucy and even stronger words with Nußknacker, who every Christmas comes marching into the drawing room as though he owned the place and takes up his stand in the fireplace from where he looks ferociously at us all. I just roar with laughter at his antics and this makes him grind his teeth – which, to his extreme annoyance, makes me laugh even more!! And then I must encourage India to face the day – she always has difficulty with this (the land of dreams is so much more inhabitable than this one!) – and generally spread light and joy about the place.

I wish you also great Joy for the Season and the New Year and congratulate you on finding such convivial and understanding friends with whom to live – not an easy task in this present degenerate world!

Viel Spaß!, viel Glück! u. Frohe Weihnachten!

Ihr

Sir Felix Bartholdy Mendelssohn

p.s. Are your eyes really yellow-gold? Mine are green like India's – in fact I am sure we are related we have so much in common – we even have the same handwriting. As I am suffering from writer's cramp, I have asked Miss Russell, in her *rôle* as my secretary, to type this for me – but you can tell – just from the signature!!

Worcester Park, 21st. December, 2007

Dear Fuchsi,

I am so pleased you like my poem *When my Lion Roars*, which, of course, I wrote and then dictated to India. As I pointed out in my last letter, so there should be no mistake, I am, in fact, not a lion but a very handsome cat, although I say it myself, she put that bit in – but, as I said before, India is a poet and one has to make allowances – they see things in a different way.

Thank you for the card – yes I do like *The Robins' Christmas* and am on very good terms with all the robins here (although I seem to remember when I was young and silly getting rather irritable with their bouncy ways!). I am, in fact, a rescinded member of the R.S.P.B. – India cancelled our joint membership when they started shooting Ruddy Ducks (ruddy people!) – not very protective we thought! She now calls it *The Royal Society for the Prevention of Birds!* Personally, I hate violence and am never happier than when the fire is crackling, Lucy (the other rescue cat who lives here, a little trying but then she had a very difficult & cruel beginning) is snoozing on the sofa and the humans are peacefully reading or writing. Fortunately there is no television here and the radio is hardly ever on so it is quite quiet, allowing for philosophical thought, as you can see from my poem.

Well, I'll conclude this short epistle and wish you a very Comfortable, Warm & Purry New Year.

Yours faithfully, (and in Cat Language 'faithful' means something!)

Felix Bartholdy Mendelssohn Bt.

A Call for Humility

to Joseph Milne

We are.
I am.
What sounding simplicity
But who can explain
Their meaning?

from *Early Poems*
India Russell

Who are we to know
who God is
how trees and birds and animals communicate
how stars live and love and die

Who are we
Who am I
Who,
as the caterpillar said,
are you?

Just stop the creaking mind awhile
and see the loving bird
within the embracing tree
the springing grass
the moving delicacy of the
spider's homespun web
the moving traceries of branches
echoing the waving leaves of
distant ocean coral

All is in all, in patterns of great harmony.
You, also, are the bird, the coral leaf,
The tree.

There is no hierarchy, the mystic,
Giordano Bruno, wrote. Divinity is in All and All is Unity.
All sings in All and we should gladly give our humble
voices to
this universal hymn of praise.

Now, as ever

but perhaps men are afraid
afraid of losing stature;

They burnt poor Giordano at the stake
For preaching such iniquity.

The Lesson

Feeling unconnected, lost
In the incomprehensible web
Of things,
I opened my desk drawer
And aimlessly pulled towards me
A large folder labelled 'To Sort'.
Yes, my whole life, I thought,
Notes, lines of verse, ideas, old photographs,
Unconnected, unresolved.

Depressed, I slowly closed the overloaded drawer
And as I did a slip of paper, on which
I'd written, 'Dr. Muffet loved spiders
Four hundred years ago', fell into my lap.
I put it back together with the rest of the
Unsorted layers of my life and
Walked out of my study
                                        alone in all the world

And there
Suspended from the ceiling, on a level
With my clouded eyes, was a large and
Vibrant spider, a being from a fairy tale,
Smiling at me with sage remonstrance.

Worcester Park, 7th. December, 2008

Dear Fuchsi,

Und wie geht es nun mit Ihnen? Wunderschön *sans doute*. Bei mir geht es auch gut – nur daß seit September ich bin hier alleine (d.h. außerdem India u. Michael). Die liebe, schöne Lucy ist am 7ten gestorben. Es ist sehr traurig gewesen aber auch sehr wunderbar.

Im August hat India eine Ansichtskarte schnell gemalt – es war der Blick vom Wohnzimmer – sie saß auf dem Sofa und malte bloß was sie durch die Balkontüren sah – Pflanze, Bäume u.s.w. und auch einen sehr schönen großen Busch. Nie hat sie sowas gemalt – und im nächsten Monat ist die schöne Lucy unter dem gleichen Busch gestorben. Die ganze Wochenende, d.h. Freitag und Samstag, hat Lucy und die Natur sich für ihres Fortgehen vorbereitet. Lucy war sehr schwach, aber Samstag früh, als eine Eule schrie und der aufmerksame Mond schimmerte, ist sie aus dem Hause, die Treppen hinunter in Richtung des Gebüsches langsam fortgegangen bis sie ihr Ziel erreichte. (India wollte sie im Hause behalten aber Lucy wußte was sie zu tun hatte.)

Und der ganze Samstag als Lucy unter ihrem Busch lag war es sonderlich leise im Garten. Ein sanfter Regen fiel und kleine Vögelein flogen in und aus dem beschützenden Strauch während oben, in dem Pflaumenbaum, ein Rotkehlchen sang mit gedämpter Stimme.

Und dann am 4Uhr Sonntag früh ist India durch die Balkontüren getreten – gleich ins Paradies, wie sie schrieb. Luft und Ort war verwandelt, zauberhaft, eine andere Welt. Ein wunderschönes Parfum, Nachtkerze und etwas seltsam und wunderbar, hing in der Luft, das sie wie ein Freund streichelte. Es war wie ein Wink vom Paradies. Am 8Uhr wann Michael in den Garten ging um Lucy nachzusehen, war sie tot. Und India wußte daß um 4.Uhr, an jene zauberhafte, parfumierte Zeit, die kleine Lucy ins Paradies hinübergegangen war.

(Please excuse errors – I am a little overwrought.)

(And how are you now? Wonderful sans doute. I am also well – only since September I have been alone here (apart from India & Michael that is.) Dear little Lucy died on the 7th. It was very sad but also very wonderful.

In August India painted a little picture – it was the view from the drawing room – she sat on the sofa and painted just what she saw through the balcony doors, plants, trees etc. and also a very beautiful large bush. Never had she painted such a thing – and in the next month Lucy died under that very bush.

For the whole weekend, i.e. Friday and Saturday, Lucy and Nature had prepared for her leaving. Lucy was very weak, but early on Saturday, as an owl hooted and the attentive moon glimmered, she slowly went out of the house, down the steps in the direction of the bush until she reached her goal. (India wanted to keep her in the house but Lucy knew what she had to do.)

And all Saturday as Lucy lay under her bush it was strangely quiet in the garden. A gentle rain was falling and the whole day long little birds were flying in and out of the sheltering shrub whilst above, in the plum tree, a robin sang with muted voice.

And then at 4 o'clock early Sunday morning India stepped through the balcony doors – straight into Paradise, as she wrote. A wonderfully beautiful perfume, evening primrose and something strange and wonderful, hung in the air that caressed her like a friend. It was like a sign from Paradise. At 8 o'clock when Michael went in the garden to see how Lucy was, she was dead. And India knew that at 4 o'clock, at that magical perfumed time, little Lucy had passed over into Paradise.)

I will now write in English as I find talking about Lucy very difficult and a change of language may help.

I'm afraid I could not continue, even in English, as I felt too moved.

Thursday Morning

I am writing this on the bed, as India came in late last night, cold, tired and rather flat, so I miaowed some encouragement and suggested she had a little mulled wine in front of the fire with me. She gratefully accepted the suggestion, put some more logs on the stove, began to relax and told me a bit about her evening.

I found it all rather odd. The Imagination, as we both know, is vital, in the real sense of the word, to humans. Without it they are automata (see E.T.A. Hoffmann); animals & the natural world have it naturally, it doesn't have to be nurtured, it's just there! But with humans one has to be careful – it can easily be swamped out of existence. Now William Blake, as we know, was a champion of the imagination – 'The Man who in his Mind and Thoughts never Travel'd to Heaven is no Artist'. (India had this on her study wall when she was a very young student). We know this is a fundamental Truth. So why did that Blake Society performance present the Man of Imagination in a way that flattened and dulled. Blake's work was not intended for performance – far better the student lose himself in the text and illustrations of Blake's *Milton* or whatever and allow the Great Mysterious Imagination to provide the spiritual projections, movements and music. And here a quick word about the music last night. I understood from India that when the Lark (dear, beautiful bird) was mentioned, the musician performed a quick lark-ascending-twiddle – quite awful, and most irritating to underline things like that, as bad as pointing to things referred to, such as parts of the body or the ground or the sky or whatever – *clichés extraordinaire*, aural and visual!! So all in all we both went to bed very late and somewhat disgruntled and I, consequently, have deviated from what I was going to tell you (now perforce briefly) about –

And that is my story *Rory in Dreamland* (to which India has appended, with my full permission, her own name.) By way of Christmas Greetings, I am sending you a facsimile of the

Endpiece to the story *Life is but a Dream*. It is a pastel by India and originally only had the Merprince and Merprincess in it but then when I looked at it I felt something was missing, so I jumped into the Magic Circle – and there I am, in my rôle of Sir Boswell, right in the middle of things, as you can see!! I hope you like the costume. Acting is in the family so I suppose it had to come out somehow!

I haven't time now to tell you the whole story – but it is very good indeed especially as I feature in it as one, if not the main character. You will have an opportunity of seeing me (in my hey-days – the story was written quite a few years ago) in formal dress escorting the Princess Greta, a Mermaid, down the Glass Staircase of Moon Palace to the Ball, on the Christmas card that India is sending your friends, the Herberts. Rory, as you can see is about to skid down the stairs despite the warning of Felix the Phosphorescent Horse who is announcing the Guests. In the background, among others, is Sir Ernest Flowers, the Serpent who holds the World together. For the Occasion of the Grand Ball, where Pegasus, Neptune and all the Gods are present, Sir Ernest has appointed a deputy to curl round the world until he can resume his duties. I tell you this in case you were worried; you can see that Rory's friends, Rufus and Robin, are looking rather nervous of Sir Ernest – quite unnecessarily as he is a Gentleman in all senses of the word. I haven't really time now to relate more of my exciting and true story, *Rory in Dreamland*, but I know you'd enjoy it particularly my chapters dealing with the Theatre of Dreamland and the Tree of Fate, Yggdrasill.

And so, until my next missive, I wish you, dear Fuchsi, a most pleasant, warm and purry Christmas & A Very Happy New Year!

Viel Spaß!

Ihr

Sir Felix Bartholdy Mendelssohn
Homme de lettres trés renommé

The Garden Party

Oh yes, I was there at that illustrious party,
Inarticulate amongst such august hosts,
Circulating, glass in hand, but only able to
admire or smile,
Painfully aware I could not contribute to such a
great occasion,
An awed and silent guest witnessing
The magnificence and ritual;
The harmonious sounds of celebration
Bearing my senses to another sphere as I walked
Shyly through the colourful throng —

Trembling delicate beauty side by side
With sturdy masculine strength,
Tentative débutantes and eager gleaming youths
Watched by knowing chaperones,
Brief flitting visitors from exotic climes,
Workers still at work but pausing now and then
to celebrate;
And then, suddenly, the joyous dancing and the games
And all around such warmth and telling vibrancy
One felt oneself to be upon the threshold of Reality.

Yes, I was there that rainy July dusk.
My faithful cat beside me,
Wandering amongst the beauty and the strength
Of trees, shrubs, birds, butterflies and bees and all the
Living world encompassed in that garden,
A wondering novice in the Realm of Truth and Beauty.

from Felix Bartholdy Mendelssohn*, Worcester Park

Jasper the Catt,
The Vicarage,
Old Malden.

4th. September, 2009

Dear Jasper,

I am so pleased there is a cat writing again in the *Old Malden News* and was most upset at the demise of your former correspondent. I and the two friends with whom I live - both humans (but one with feline potential!) have read the magazine since we moved here some years ago and have found it most interesting and encouraging, yes, that is the right word I think, as not one of us is conventional in belief, apart from the fact that we see divinity in All and, like Giordano Bruno, (was he a cat do you think?) cannot accept the notion of a hierachy in or a division between mankind and the natural world. If only humans would be silent and still and contemplate a tree or a garden in the rain or, like your reverend friend, Kevin Scott, a beautiful stained glass window, they would begin to 'see thro' not with the eye' as William Blake wrote. I do it all the time particularly as I have now reached the age of discretion! There is too much clamour, too much chatter, and too much 'soul-searching', yes that is the expression hackneyed but apt, in the human world. If only they would let Nature, not man-manipulated but real nature, speak to them, like St. Francis, there would be far less anger and pride and fear amongst them.

I am sending, by way of support to my arguement, two poems written (ostensibly) by India Russell, one of my companions here, but in fact mostly dictated by myself.

I'm afraid this letter does not constitute a question apart from the obvious one – why does the Church say man is the guardian of Nature when, I experience, and believe it to be the opposite or, in more liberal frame of mind, symbiotic!?

With very best wishes,

Yours sincerely

Felix (Veteran of the Parish of Cuddington)

p.s. I do hope you like the poems, particularly *When my lion roars*. In fact I am not a lion but a rather lovely, large long-haired tabby cat with a curly tummy and very fine whiskers – but India does get rather carried away by her imagination!

* There is story behind this!

Ask Jasper

Dear Felix-Bartholdy-Mendelssohn
(cat of the parish of Cuddington)

Thank you for your encouraging letter which deserves a longer reply than this. Your question was: "Why does the Church say Man is the guardian of Nature when I experience it to be the opposite?"

Short answer: because the Church has an extraordinary capacity for being spectacularly wrong.

Less short answer: because the writer of Genesis 1.28 put into the mouth of God the words to Adam: 'have dominion over every living thing.'
Sadly, up until the 20th. Century the Church didn't just interpret this as 'take care of them': it understood it to mean 'nature is there for you to do with it as you wish.'
Even the idea of humans being 'guardians of nature' is a bit arrogant, when you consider how much they depend on the rest of us.

Every time the Bible says, 'and God said', Christians have got to decide whether they are going to take it at face value or not.
The consequences for the rest of us - not to mention lots of humans – can be pretty disastrous.

Jasper

Old Malden News November 2009

WORCESTER HOUSE
Surrey

from Sir Felix Bartholdy Mendelssohn, V.B.A.,F.R.S.C.

4th. November, 2009

Dear Fuchsi,

My dear friend India has told me about your lovely photographs that your dear friend Jack showed her. I'm afraid I do not have any to send to you – India is so old-fashioned you know - she simply hates computers and watches and things so I suppose she doesn't like cameras either!! (And I haven't even seen a television – for which blessing, though, I am most grateful!)

Anyway, I'm not writing to you to tell you about all the things we do not have here – but to tell you that I have written to the local Vicarage Cat, Jasper, who has a question page in the Church Magazine. He holds a high editorial position on the publication *Old Malden News*. Old Malden is very ancient, by the way; recent excavations have revealed very early settlements nearby and even the church dates back to Saxon times. Anyway, Jasper answers readers' questions – theological and otherwise and so I wrote to him on a subject that has always puzzled me. I enclose a copy of my letter and his reply printed in this month's issue which, although perforce brief, I thought pretty good. I had always known they had got in wrong in the Bible about man having 'dominion' over animals!! What nonsense!!

I can see from your photographs that you are enjoying the peak of health. As for myself – considering my (I have to admit it) advanced age, I feel very well. The rheumatic back leg is annoying but not too painful, due to regular doses of Rhus. Tox. and although I sometimes think of the scampering days of my youth, I am most pleased now to doze on the sofa and listen to the quiet pages of a book or writing pad being turned and glimpse the flickering shadows cast by the fire. Good books they are as well, most accommodating, – I have slept on many of them in my time but now find cushions more comfortable!

I trust you enjoyed my previous epistle sent some time ago.

Well, I will conclude now and wish you a cosy and delightful winter together with your dear friends at No. 34, and remain

Yours purringly,

Felix

Under Bombardment

We were under bombardment again last night,
Being November, that month which heralds the
Heralding time of Advent and the Peacebringer.
We took shelter in the drawing room and books
And lit the fire to drive away our fear.

Brave Felix crawled beneath the chaise into his dug-out
While I stretched out upon it as chief fire-watcher,
And read the shining poetry of Borges
And the writings of that other stunning war of Owen's
And drank *Graves*.

At eleven o'clock there was a temporary cease-fire
Due maybe to the drumming rain, falling as a
Gift from Heaven and the watching Gods.
Felix wanted to go out and, contrary to all black-out restrictions,
I switched on the floodlight and, donning mackintosh and hat,
Went with him down into the garden.

Only a minute breathing the divine washed innocent air
In company with the trees and shocked and waiting birds
Then in again to shelter just in time.
Guiltily I turned the floodlight off and resumed converse
With Wilfred Owen, Felix and with Borges,
The fire flickering in ancient knowing harmony with our minds.

I hope we won't receive a reprimand
From the authorities,
For spilling light.

The Leaf

Sitting in the spoon-back chair
Whose lines and mellow craftmanship
Are always pleasing,
Transported dreamily back to childhood
By the summoning scent of lilac
I gazed upon a leaf, back-lit
By the table lamp;

And suddenly, I awakened into yet another
World of singing and harmonious wonder,
For here were forking paths, strange lights,
Beautiful designs,
A speaking pattern beyond thought and craft,
A world of mystery
Beyond our human compass;

And returning to the confines of the present room,
I wondered yet again how man

Could think himself the measure of all things
In the pure light of one single leaf of lilac.

ORCHARD GATE

from Sir Felix Bartholdy Mendelssohn, S.P., F.R.S.C.*

27th. September, 2012

Dear Dr. Cross,

My dear friend and private secretary, India, was delighted to receive a copy of the now famous portrait of myself with mask. Yes, I certainly was in Pisa, as a guest of Lord Byron at the Palazzo Lanfranchi. I have often told her about that memorable sitting at the Palazzo. Artists had been fighting for the privilege to have me sit for them (or, as it turned out, stand!) and so I asked dear George to make the choice, I, of course, being too occupied with Affairs of the Spirit. And I must say the result is most satisfactory. Good colour, good expression and just the right amount of mystery (for the human eye, that is.).

And then came the clamorous requests for the picture, from kings and princes. Being mainly of the ethereal world and not requiring possessions, it was of little interest to me who should own it, although I understand it now hangs in Florence. Although so many humans think otherwise, we own nothing in this fleeting world apart from our Imagination and the Ability to fly beyond time into the Great Reality – and they are, of course, intangible!

Being now towards the end of my sojourn in this clangorous world, through which I have lent a helping paw to India and Michael, it is good to purr on the sofa and reflect on my experiences. The Grand Tour was only one of many. I knew Bastet, you know, in Egypt. Now there's a place! The music of the spheres, not to mention the singing pyramids, surrounded one with celestial rhythm. That same rhythm which Shelley heard. I had a lot in common with Percy, so much so that I often took him for a feline – such fluid movement, such indifference to the material and such pure insight into the world of the spirit. Many, many times we have purred and nodded together by the fire where sometimes I would fall asleep on the manuscript of his latest poem – he always took this to mean that it was indeed expressing the inexpressible! (I do hope you enjoy India's paper on the subject. She has read it to me several times and I have given it my Full Seal of Approval!).

Thank you so much for reminding me of that particularly rich experience in Pisa with Byron and Shelley. Both loved the animal world, which is, as we know, the world of the spirit, and abhorred blood sports, and not only on humanitarian grounds. 'This amusement of shooting,' Shelley once wrote to Hogg, 'familiarises people with the society of inferiors and the gross and harsh habits belonging to those sort of pursuits.'

And there are enough 'gross and harsh habits' in this world. As Ibsen wrote, men must strive towards a 'spiritual aristocracy' of which I and my fellow aristocrats are representatives!

Well, I shall now muse further on my experiences and travels and then have a good sleep full of dreams!

With all good wishes and felicitations,

I remain,

Felix
Sir Felix Bartholdy Mendlessohn

***Society of Pan, Fellow of the Royal Society of Cats**

They all knew

I didn't need to tell the bees
That he had died,
Their parting song was humming through the garden
As we brought him out.

I didn't need to tell the pigeons of his death
For they were cooing him a final lullaby
As the evening primrose sent its balmy
Perfume through the air.

I didn't need to tell the darkening sky of
Felix's passing,
The lone bird hanging motionless above his grave
Cried out to all the heavens at his burial.

I didn't need to tell the blackbird or his young ones that
Gentle Felix would no longer wander wonderingly in the
garden
For they had come and left a feather on his grave by our
offerings of
Roses and of lavender and rosemary.

I didn't need to tell the rhododendron
And the weeping bushes round his grave
Or the robins or the squirrels or the guardian trees
For they knew, they knew

They all knew and mourned
And then gave celebratory thanks for
his so great
and ever loving gentle soul.

Endpiece to *Rory in Dreamland* with Felix in his rôle of Sir Boswell written and illustrated by India Russell

INDIA RUSSELL

recent publications and lectures

POETRY
published widely. from 2000
Much of her work is concerned with spiritual dimensions, particularly with regard to the natural world and man's relation to it.

COLLECTIONS

The Kaleidoscope of Time	Stacey International	2007
		reprinted 2008, 2010
The Dance of Life	Godstow Press	2010
The Lane to Paradise - Felix A Celebration	private circulation	2013
Pattern & The Golden Thread	Paekakariki Press	2014

ARTICLES

Murder Weekends in the Golden Past
India Russell takes a one-way ticket to St Mary Mead *Connections* Autumn 2002

The Devil and the Deep Blue Sea
India Russell examines three plays which exemplify drama on the emotional edge *Connections* Autumn 2003

PAPERS

Friedrich Hölderlin — Lightning Conductor of the Divine

presented to	The Temenos Academy	November	2007
published in	*Temenos Academy Review*		2008

Expressing the Inexpressible: Henrik Ibsen and Isadora Duncan

presented to	The Temenos Academy	October	2012
published in	*Temenos Academy Review*		2014

Studies in Loneliness, or 'zwei unbehauste Menschen.'
The Tragic Destinies of Hedda Gabler and Effi Briest
presented to The Fontane-Kreis Großbritannien und Irland May 2014

THEATRE

The Secret Rooms of the Mind
Dance Drama for performer & musician written, choreographed & performed by India Russell. Freebird 1994-5

with grateful thanks to Felix

***

India Russell read German and Norwegian at University College London and was junior research fellow in German at King's College. She is a Licentiate of Guildhall School of Music & Drama in Drama, Speech & Prosody.